Praise for
The Fix-It Friends: *Have No Fear!*

"Fears are scary! But don't worry: the Fix-It Friends know how to vanquish all kinds of fears, with humor and step-by-step help. Nicole C. Kear has written a funny and helpful series."

—Fran Manushkin, author of the Katie Woo series

"Full of heart and more than a little spunk, this book teaches kids that fear stands no chance against friendship and courage. Where were the Fix-It Friends when I was seven years old?"

—Kathleen Lane, author of *The Best Worst Thing*

"I love the Fix-It Friends as a resource to give to the families I work with. The books help kids see their own power to overcome challenges—and they're just plain fun to read."

—Lauren Knickerbocker, PhD, Co-Director, Early Childhood Service, NYU Child Study Center

"Hooray for these young friends who work together; this diverse crew will have readers looking forward to more."

—*Kirkus Reviews*

The Fix-It Friends
The Show Must Go On

Nicole C. Kear
illustrated by **Tracy Dockray**

[Imprint]
MAKE YOUR MARK

NEW YORK

A part of Macmillan Publishing Group, LLC
175 Fifth Avenue, New York, NY 10010

THE FIX-IT FRIENDS: THE SHOW MUST GO ON. Text copyright © 2017 by
Nicole C. Kear. Illustrations copyright © 2017 by Imprint. All rights reserved. Printed
in the United States of America by LSC Communications, Harrisonburg, Virginia.

Library of Congress Cataloging-in-Publication Data

Names: Kear, Nicole C., author. | Dockray, Tracy, illustrator.
Title: The Fix-It Friends: the show must go on / Nicole C. Kear ; illustrations by
Tracy Dockray.
Other titles: Show must go on
Description: First edition. | New York : Imprint, 2017. | Series: The Fix-It Friends ; [3] |
Summary: When Veronica joins the second grade Drama Club, she meets Liv,
who needs the Fix-It Friends' help to prepare for opening night.
Identifiers: LCCN 2016056986 (print) | LCCN 2017027702 (ebook) |
ISBN 9781250086693 (Ebook) | ISBN 9781250115751 (hardcover) |
ISBN 9781250086686 (pbk.)
Subjects: | CYAC: Theater—Fiction. | Dyslexia—Fiction. | Helpfulness—Fiction. |
Brothers and sisters—Fiction. | Friendship—Fiction. | Schools—Fiction.
Classification: LCC PZ7.1.K394 (ebook) | LCC PZ7.1.K394 Fju 2017 (print) |
DDC [Fic]—dc23
LC record available at https://lccn.loc.gov/2016056986

Our books may be purchased in bulk for promotional, educational, or business use.
Please contact your local bookseller or the Macmillan Corporate and Premium
Sales Department at (800) 221-7945 ext. 5442 or by e-mail at
MacmillanSpecialMarkets@macmillan.com.

Book design by Ellen Duda
Illustrations by Tracy Dockray
Imprint logo designed by Amanda Spielman

First edition, 2017

ISBN 978-1-250-11575-1 (hardcover)

1   3   5   7   9   10   8   6   4   2

ISBN 978-1-250-08668-6 (paperback)

1   3   5   7   9   10   8   6   4   2

ISBN 978-1-250-08669-3 (ebook)

mackids.com

Nothing good comes to those who steal,
but especially terrible things come to those who steal books.
I should know. I, Eleanor Tibbs, devised the punishment myself.
Proceed with caution.

For Valentina, queen of my heart

With special thanks to consultant Susan Barton, founder
of Bright Solutions for Dyslexia
www.BrightSolutions.us

Chapter 1

I'm Veronica Conti and I'm seven.

Seven and a half, actually.

I think I may even be seven and three-quarters, but my know-it-all brother, Jude, says I'm not.

He is nine years old, which is only two years older than me, but he is always correcting me and bossing me around and trying to help me when I don't even need help!

When I tell people I'm seven and three-quarters, Jude says, "You won't be seven and three-quarters until December. That's just simple fractions, which you don't know how to do yet."

"I may not know fractions, but I know percents!" I reply. "I know that you are one hundred percent annoying."

He shrugs. "Just trying to help."

My best friend, Cora, already knows how to do fractions even though she is in second grade, just like me. She's a whiz at math . . . and spelling . . . and pretty much everything in school, except for gym and music. She finishes her homework with lightning speed and never needs any help.

It takes me forever to do the same homework. I don't mind my reading, because I get to choose any book I want. I love books about animals. Especially talking animals! Especially talking animals with superpowers!

But the rest of my homework is so boring that I have to take a little break after every question

The Show Must Go On

to sing or doodle or do a handstand. Some of the questions don't make any sense, and it feels like a Martian made them up. I just skip those.

Then, after a million minutes, Jude walks by and says, "Are you *still* doing your homework? I finished mine ages ago!" It drives me bonkers.

Then my mom or dad or grandma or grandpa

walks by and says, "Need some help?" But I shake my head because if Jude can do it by himself, then so can I.

I tap my fingers on my desk really fast, which is what I do when I'm thinking hard, and *finally* I finish my homework sheet. I jump for joy. Then my mom or dad or grandma or grandpa checks it and says, "Why'd you leave all these questions blank? And didn't you see the back of the sheet?" I get so frustrated that I feel like snapping my pencil in half.

In fact, I did that once. You know, pencils are not that hard to break. In fact, they're pretty flimsy.

After I broke the pencil, I told my mom, "I'm so bad at homework! Jude finished his hours ago, all by himself."

My mom is really good at knowing just what to say when I'm upset. That's because she's a therapist and part of her job is to help people with their feelings.

"What's wrong with needing a little help?" she asked. "After all, you help people all the time."

That's true. I *am* the president of the Fix-It Friends. The group has four members—me, Cora, Jude, and his best friend, Ezra—and the whole point of our group is to help kids with their problems.

"But that's *real-life* problems," I said. "Like worry and teasing and stuff. Not subtraction problems and what's-the-capital-of-Kentucky problems."

"It's the same thing," Mom said.

I sighed.

"What you have to remember," said Mom, "is that homework may be easier for Jude, but there are plenty of things that are hard for him that are easy for you."

"That's for sure! Have you ever heard Jude sing?

He sounds like a dying hyena. And he can't do anything on the monkey bars. If he tries to hang by his knees, his legs get all tangled and Ezra has to rescue him."

"And all those things are easy for you," Mom pointed out.

"Oh yeah," I agreed. "I could do that stuff in my sleep!"

Sometimes I *actually* do that stuff in my sleep. Then Jude, who sleeps in the top bunk, says very

angrily, "You're singing in your sleep again! SNAP OUT OF IT!"

What a grump.

"It's that way with everyone, you know," Mom said. "We all have stuff we struggle with."

I nodded, but the truth was, I didn't really believe her, because some people just seem perfect, with absolutely no problems at all.

Like Liv.

Chapter 2

I met Liv at Drama Club. Glorious, marvelous Drama Club!

Here's how I heard about Drama Club:

It was right after Thanksgiving break, at the end of the school day. My wonderful teacher, Miss Mabel, was handing out forms and flyers for us to take home.

One of the flyers caught my eye because it was printed on bright red paper. This is what it said:

The Show Must Go On

CALLING ALL DRAMA QUEENS AND KINGS!!

Do you love soaking up the spotlight?

Join the second-grade Drama Club!

Who: You! And me, Ginger Frost, your director.

What: We'll be performing (drumroll, please) . . .

Alice in Wonderland!

Where: The auditorium

When: November 26–December 19

Mondays and Wednesdays 3–4:30 p.m.

Why: Because it's LOADS OF FUN!

Auditions will be held at our first meeting.

Everyone who wants to participate will get a part.

Remember, there are no small parts,

only small actors!

We need students of all ages to help with lights,

sets, and costumes. See Miss Tibbs for details.

After I read that flyer, I squealed with delight and showed it to Cora, who sits at my table.

She was so excited that she spun around in a circle, and her twirly skirt flew up in the air. So did her red curls, which looked exactly like a bunch of red Slinkys attached to her head.

I knew Cora would be excited about making costumes. She's always giving makeovers to everyone—especially her twin sister, Camille, who likes to wear sweatpants and basketball jerseys and hates combing her hair worse than I hate homework.

I really don't like it when Cora gives me a make-over, because she always stuffs me into a tight, poofy dress that chokes and itches me and makes me feel like a doll that has come to life, like in some horror movie.

I figured it would be good for her to do make-overs on someone else for a change, and that's why I showed her the Drama Club flyer.

"Costumes!" she chirped, in her squeaky parakeet voice.

"Acting!" I exclaimed.

"Perfect!" we both said together. Then we did our secret handshake. Well, I call it a *hand*shake, but really it uses a lot more than just hands. Of course

I can't possibly say another word about it, because then it wouldn't be a secret anymore, would it?

On the first day of Drama Club, I wore my most dramatic outfit to school: black leggings with a black turtleneck. My grandmother who lives upstairs, Nana, even let me tie her silky black scarf over my hair like an old-fashioned movie star.

Jude glanced up at me from the kitchen table, where he was reading a book, like he does every morning. This one was called *The Maniacal Mutants of Mars*.

He tipped his chin down and looked at me over the tops of his tortoiseshell eyeglasses.

"Why are you dressed like a ninja?" he asked.

I glared at him.

"I know! I know!" said Dad, raising his hand up high and pretending to be a little kid answering a question at school. Dad is so funny. He's the family clown. Well, him and my little sister, Pearl.

"Yes, Dad?" I pretended to be the teacher calling on him.

"You're dressed like a serious actor because today is the first day of Drama Club!"

Mom walked in then, sipping coffee and brushing her hair. It is blond like mine and Jude's and Pearl's, but hers is dyed. I remember the first time I found out her hair was dyed. I burst into tears.

"No, Mommy!" Mini-Me had wailed. "I don't want your hair to die!"

What can I say? I was in preschool then, and I had a lot of strange ideas about things.

Mom brushed her dyed-but-still-alive hair and gulped coffee.

"Ooooh, first day of Drama Club," she said. "Very exciting."

Jude stopped eating his breakfast. He doesn't eat cereal, like a normal person. He eats yogurt. The plain kind. With dried cranberries in it. Bleeyygch.

"Oh yeah, I heard about Drama Club. Ezra's

helping with the lights," he said. "Miss Tibbs asked me to help with the sets."

Miss Tibbs is a super-strict recess and lunch teacher who also may possibly be a witch. Here's why I think so:

1. She always wears black, from her eyeglasses all the way down to her shoes. And she is not an actor.

2. She knows absolutely everything about all the kids in the school. Even their deepest secrets. She even knows Jude's middle name. *No one* knows that!

3. She always has an angry expression on her face, like she just ate something really, really sour.

All the kids skitter away when Miss Tibbs walks down the hall. If you go near her, you'll get in big trouble—even if you aren't doing anything wrong! The only kids who don't skitter away are Jude and Cora. That's because they are Mr. and Miss Perfect and Miss Tibbs adores them. So I wasn't surprised that she had asked Jude to help with the sets.

"I heard that Ms. Frost is the real deal," Jude said, taking a bite of his yogurt. "A professional actor."

"I wonder if Ginger Frost is her real name," I said. "It sounds too beautiful to be real."

Jude shrugged. "All I know is that Miss Tibbs says she's really talented. She saw Ms. Frost perform in *Macbeth* last year."

My mom absolutely loves Shakespeare and has told us all about his plays. *Macbeth* is her favorite. It sounds cool because it has witches and ghosts and tons and tons of blood in it. I love the character of Lady Macbeth because she is evil and blood-thirsty. I'm a sucker for villains. There is one part Mom told me about where she goes totally bonkers and thinks she has blood all over her hands, even though she doesn't. She keeps washing her hands and shouting, "Out, darn blood spot! Out, I say! GET OFF OF ME!"

Mom interrupted my thoughts: "Have you decided which part you want to be in *Alice in Wonderland*?"

I put my hands on my hips, scrunched up my eyebrows, and shouted, "Off with her head!"

"Of course you want to be the Queen of Hearts," muttered Jude. "All she does is yell and boss people around."

I wanted to dunk his face in his bowl so it would be covered with yogurt, like a clown who got a pie thrown in his face, only a lot less tasty.

Instead I asked Mom and Dad, "Did you like the way I said that line? Because I could do it differently."

I tried out a whole bunch of choices.

I said it with an Italian accent, like Nana: "Off-a with-a her head-a!"

I said it like a teenager, pretending to chew gum and twirl my hair: "Like, off with her head?"

I said it scared, with my eyes wide, in a whisper: "Off with her h-h-head?"

Just then I heard a tiny voice say, "Off wiffer 'ED!" A moment later, a tiny face peeked out around the corner.

"Pearly Pie!" I exclaimed.

Pearl ran into the kitchen,

with her wispy blond hair sticking straight up. She held her stuffed rat, Ricardo, in her arms and her paci in her hand. She was wearing one-piece pj's that were covered with cute little owls—or, as Pearl calls them, "ow-wows."

She chanted, "Off wiffer 'ed, off wiffer 'ed, off wiffer 'ed!"

Mom and Dad and Jude and I all laughed.

"Good thing Pearl's not in the second grade," said Dad. "Or you'd have some stiff competition."

Chapter 3

That afternoon, at three o'clock exactly, I darted out of my classroom like an arrow and flew to the auditorium. I thought for sure I'd be the first person there.

But when I threw open the big brown door, I saw there was someone already there. She was standing in the middle of the stage, and this is what she looked like:

1. Lots of thick black hair, cut short with bangs.

2. Enormous blue eyes with enormous lashes.

The Show Must Go On

3. Little silver hoop earrings in her ears.

The black-haired, blue-eyed, hoop-earringed girl was standing still in the middle of the stage, with her head tilted like she was thinking very hard. Then, suddenly, she clutched her chest with her hand and made a hideous howl.

I ran over to the stage and asked, "Are you okay?"

She flashed me a big, beaming smile and nodded. Then she went back to clutching her chest

and howling and staggering around the stage. She walked one way, then changed directions, and the whole time she was on her tiptoes.

Ohhhhh, I thought. *She's just acting! It's a death scene!*

I sat down in the front row to watch.

The girl fell forward onto one knee. Then she fell backward onto her back very gracefully, with both legs straight up in the air. Then she put her legs down and got really still.

I thought the scene was over, so I clapped loudly, but suddenly, she stuck her legs back up in the air and gave a bunch of fast kicks. Then she turned her face right to me, said, "So long!" and shut her eyes.

I clapped again, and the girl popped up onto her feet. She raised her arms over her head and did three ballet spins in a row without stopping. Then she took a deep bow.

"That was wonderful!" I gushed.

"Thanks," she said. "I practice all the time—when I'm not practicing ballet. This morning, I did five different death scenes before breakfast."

The girl hopped down the steps of the stage in little pretty ballet jumps, and then she walked over to where I was sitting.

"But there are no death scenes in *Alice in Wonderland*, are there?" I asked.

"Nah. But it's very handy to have a death scene ready to show off how dramatic you can be. That was my Shot-by-an-Arrow scene. I can also do a Hit-by-a-Bowling-Ball one and a Getting-Bit-by-a-Vampire and lots of others, too."

Then the girl did something amazing; she

stuck her foot up on the stage and leaned to stretch sideways over it. She was as bendy as a piece of taffy!

"What's your name, and what part do you want to be in the play?" she asked.

The girl put her stretched-out leg on the floor and stuck the other foot up on the stage.

The Show Must Go On

"I'm Veronica," I said, "and I want to be the Queen of Hearts."

"Oooooh, that will be so fun," the girl said. "I want to be Alice. My name's Olivia Oikonomopoulous."

"*What's* your name?"

"Olivia Oikonomopoulous."

"Can you say it one more time?"

"Olivia Oikonomopoulous. But everyone calls me Liv."

"That's a lot easier to remember," I said, breathing out a sigh of relief. "You have a really long name."

"Tell me about it. The whole thing all together is twenty-one letters. So I never, ever write my whole name out on homework and notebooks and stuff!"

I giggled.

"But I do like my name," said Liv. "I'm named after my great-grandmother. My mom says the name Olivia is from Shakespeare."

"I love Shakespeare!" I squealed. "Even though I've never actually read any of it."

Liv smiled. "My last name comes from my dad. I have no idea what it means because it's Greek and I don't really speak Greek. I just know how to say *yes* and *no* and *thanks* and *opa*!"

"*Opa?*" I repeated. "What does that mean?"

"It sort of means 'hooray' or 'yay,' but you mostly use it when someone is dancing or when someone makes a mistake, like if they break a glass by accident. It kind of means 'It's okay! You made a mistake, but so what? Yippee!'"

"That's a good word for me to learn because

The Show Must Go On

I'm always breaking stuff and making mistakes," I told her. "My brother says I'm a magnet for trouble, but I always tell him it's a good thing because we have a problem-solving club. If I didn't get into trouble, we might run out of work to do!"

Liv laughed. Then, all of a sudden, she did a perfect split! She just slid right down to the floor with one leg in front and one in back, like it was the easiest thing in the world!

I have been trying to do a split in gymnastics for a whole year. I keep getting a little lower to the ground, but it is still not a full split. I couldn't believe Liv could do it so easily!

I already thought Liv was amazing, but after her perfect split, I thought she could do absolutely anything. If she had told me she could fly, or walk through walls, or turn broccoli into whipped cream with a wave of her hand, I would have believed her.

So I was really surprised by what happened next.

Chapter 4

The auditorium filled up with second graders, including a lot of my friends.

My friend Minnie walked in, holding sheets of music. I have been friends with Minnie since we were toddlers. She sits at my table in class, and she also plays tag with me pretty much every day at recess. Minnie is almost as tall as Jude, and she always wears her hair in two braids, which she chews on when she gets nervous.

"Hi, Minnie!" I said as she sat down next to me. "What part do you want to play?"

"I don't want to play a part." She smiled. "I want to play a piano!"

Minnie has been playing the piano since she was a little tiny creature, so now she is an expert. Her fingers move so fast when she plays that it almost seems like a magic trick.

Then Cora's twin sister, Camille, walked in. I knew it was her even before I turned my head to look. Camille stomps when she walks like she is wearing bricks on the bottoms of her shoes. *Clomp, clomp, clomp.*

Camille may look exactly like my best friend, with the same red, curly hair and freckles, but she's totally different from Cora in every other way.

Camille plopped down next to Minnie.

"Who do you want to be in the play?" I asked Camille.

"Oh, I don't really care," she said in her deep, raspy voice. "I'm just here because Cora's doing the costumes and Mom can't pick me up till four thirty. I figure I'll audition for something since I have to be here anyway and it's too cold to play basketball."

Just then, we heard a loud *click clack click clack* sound coming from the door to the auditorium. We all looked up and saw . . . Ginger Frost!

She looked like a real movie star. Here's why:

The Fix-It Friends

1. White coat with big fur collar.

2. Lipstick as red as a bowl of cherries.

3. Hair that twirled into twisty locks. It looked like a whole bunch of fairies had spent all night twirling her hair.

4. And that *click clack click clack* sound was from high heels! They sort of looked like the ruby slippers, only with taller heels.

"Holy cannoli," I whispered.

"You can say *that* again," whispered Liv.

"That again," I said. That cracked us both up.

Ginger Frost *click clack*ed right onto the middle of

the stage and announced, "Who's ready to make magic?"

My mouth dropped open. She talked like the queen of England!

"She's *British*!" Liv whispered in my ear.

"I *know*!"

Ginger Frost sat down right on the edge of the stage and crossed her legs. Her shiny red shoes twinkled in the light.

"That's what the theater is, you know—it's magic. We start off as girls and boys, and we become queens and rabbits and enchanted flowers. Over the next few weeks, we will transform this stage. By the time your mums and dads and mates come to see the show, they won't feel like they are in a school anymore. They'll feel as if they're in Wonderland."

It was hard to pay attention to what Ginger

Frost was saying because I was too busy staring at her hands. She moved her hands so much that it seemed like they were doing a pretty little dance. I almost got hypnotized.

"So I'll pass out scripts. Then we'll queue up in the wings, and you'll each have a go reading the part you want to play."

I shot my hand up and said, "Ms. Frost?"

She laughed a little chuckle that sounded like jingly Christmas bells.

"You can call me Ginger, love."

"Ginger," I said. "What's a queue? Did we have to bring one with us? I didn't bring anything."

She laughed again.

"Sorry. I've got a funny way of talking, haven't I? That's because I'm from London. *Queue up* is just our way of saying 'get in a line.'"

The Show Must Go On

I shot my hand up again, and Ginger nodded in my direction.

"What wings are you talking about? I didn't bring any of those, either."

Then Ginger explained that *wings* was a theater word that meant the sides of the stage, where the audience can't see you.

Then she handed out scripts, and we all scrambled into the wings to get in line.

A few kids I didn't know went first and read the parts of the Caterpillar and the Mad Hatter and the March Hare. Camille read the part of the White Rabbit in her deep rumbly voice, and Minnie played a song on the piano that sounded like a flock of sparrows singing to one another.

Then it was Liv's turn. She twirled onto the stage and introduced herself. But then she got a very nervous look on her face as she stared hard at the script without saying anything. She tapped her foot a few times. Then she swallowed a big gulp of air and started to read.

"I won . . . wonder . . ."

Liv's lower lip trembled like she was about to burst into tears. I was so surprised because Liv did *not* seem like the kind of girl to get stage fright.

The Show Must Go On

Ginger spoke up: "Just take your time, love. You're doing great."

Liv nodded. She looked at the script and blinked a whole bunch of times.

"I wonder if . . . if I've . . . needed . . . I wonder if I've been . . ." She trailed off.

Ginger spoke up again. "I've got a thought, love. Why don't we bring the next person up here, and we'll come back to you in a few minutes?"

Liv nodded really fast.

"And remember, everyone," announced Ginger, "there are loads of lovely nonspeaking roles, like the flowers and the playing cards."

Liv made a grimace, and I could tell she did *not* want to be a playing card. But I couldn't think about that, because guess whose turn was next? Mine!

I walked right into the middle of the stage in big steps.

"My name is Veronica Laverne Conti!" I said with a lot of pep. "I would like to try out for the Queen of Hearts. It's the perfect part for me because my whole family says I am a loudmouth!"

Then I read the scene, and it was the most fun ever! The best part was when I screeched "Off with her head!" and everybody laughed really loudly. I felt like a million bucks.

I was so happy that I skipped into the wings. I was happy for about ten seconds, until I saw who was waiting to go next.

Matthew Sawyer, that's who.

Matthew Sawyer is the biggest pest in the second grade. He acts like it is his job to bother me. Trust me, he is *very* good at his job.

The Show Must Go On

He was wearing a striped shirt like he always does. His shoelaces were untied, like they always are. And he was rubbing the back of his buzz-cut hair, which is what he does every time he's hatching a devilish plan.

"What are *you* doing here?" I grumbled.

"I go to school here," he said. His favorite game is playing dumb.

"I mean, what are you doing at Drama Club?"

"This is Drama Club?" he asked, pretending to be bewildered. "I thought it was Tapeworm Music Club. I brought my tapeworm with me. He plays electric guitar."

I glowered and growled at the same time.

"Matthew Sawyer! Don't you dare audition for this play!"

"News alert! This just in! Veronica Conti is

NOT the Boss of the World," he said. Then Ginger called out, "Next!" and he went right onstage.

"I'm Matt and I want to be the Cheshire Cat."

That figured. The Cheshire Cat is the most annoying character in the whole play. All he does is say nonsense. Perfect for Matthew Sawyer!

While he was reading the Cheshire Cat scene, Liv came up to me. She was biting her lip.

"Remember how you said you and your friends could fix problems?" she whispered. "Is that really true?"

I nodded.

"Then I need your help," she said. "Right *now*."

Chapter 5

"What's the matter?" I asked Liv. "Do you have stage fright?"

"No!" she said, shaking her head. "I love being onstage! I just have trouble reading."

"Ohhhh," I said. "What kind of trouble?"

"It's sort of hard to explain," she said, "but it's called dyslexia and basically it's really hard for me to sound out words I don't know. So it takes a long time for me to read something new, and right now, it can't take me a long time! I have to get the part of Alice!"

Then she grabbed both my hands with both her hands, and she looked really hard into my eyes.

"It's my dream, Veronica," she said.

Here's the thing: It's my dream come true to make someone else's dream come true. I did it one time—when my dad took us to a video arcade, and Pearl desperately wanted to win a stuffed animal from one of those grabber machines with the big metal claw. I wiggled that claw like crazy, grabbed a fluffy purple dolphin, and kept hanging on to it the whole time as the claw went up. When I handed that dolphin to Pearl, she looked so happy, I thought she'd burst. That made me overjoyed, too.

So when Liv asked me to help make her dream come true, I promised to try. Only problem was, I had no idea how.

The Show Must Go On

Then, before I knew it, I heard Ginger's voice call, "Liv? Ready to give it another go?"

That's when I got my genius idea. They don't call me the president of the Fix-It Friends for nothing. Well, actually, nobody calls me that. But they should.

"Go!" I whispered to Liv. "Stand close to the wings. I'll whisper the words to you!"

Liv sashayed onto the stage, and I crouched down behind the curtain as close to Liv as I could get.

I whispered Alice's lines slowly: "I wonder if I've been changed in the night."

"I wonder if I've been changed in the night," Liv repeated.

My plan was working!

I kept on reading and Liv kept on repeating,

until Camille walked over and asked if I wanted to go to the bathroom with her.

I shook my head and told her, "Watch out—the toilet was all clogged before."

Before I knew what was happening, Liv was repeating after me, in a very dramatic voice: "Watch out! The toilet was all clogged before!"

I gasped and whispered to Liv, "I wasn't talking to you!"

The Show Must Go On

And she gasped and repeated, "I wasn't talking to you!"

Ginger asked in a confused voice, "Have you lost your place?"

That's when Liv realized she had been saying the wrong things. Alice in Wonderland never talks about clogged toilets in the play. Not even once. They probably don't even have toilets in Wonderland. When you stop to think about it, poor Alice

probably had to pee the whole trip. No wonder she was so glad to get home!

Liv replied to Ginger, "Sorry! I don't know *what* I was thinking!"

Then she looked right at me, with a look that said, *Hey! You're making my nightmares come true instead of my dreams! Pay attention!*

And I sure did, for the rest of the scene.

When Liv was done, Ginger clapped. "That was smashing!"

Then Liv ran offstage, smiling even bigger than the Cheshire Cat.

Chapter 6

That night for dinner, Dad made chicken nuggets—or, as Pearl likes to call them, "chicky snuggles." Pearl loves chicken nuggets! Not to eat but to play with.

She likes to line a whole bunch of them up on her plate. Then she acts like her napkin is a blanket and tucks the nuggets in. She even sings them a lullaby!

But when Mom or Dad says, "Eat your chicken, Pearl," she says, "Shhhhh! They sleepin'!"

I'm too old to play with my food, of course, but

when there is ketchup, I cannot resist sticking my fingers in it and pretending I'm bleeding.

"Ahhhhh! Call a doctor!" I screeched. "My finger!"

I remembered the part from *Macbeth*, so I rubbed my hands together and shrieked, "Get out, darn blood spot! Out, I say!"

The Show Must Go On

Pearl copied me, of course: "Go 'way, you bad spot!"

Jude's best friend, Ezra, was over for dinner, and he laughed. I love it when Ezra comes over. Here's why:

1. He always gives me a part in the movies he makes with Jude. This is how I got good at acting.

2. He records me singing on his laptop so I can make a demo album. This is how I got good at singing.

3. He tells hilarious stories about Ziggy, his guinea pig who is a genius and does tricks.

4. Best of all, when Ezra is around, Jude is less bossy and annoying.

So when I pretended the ketchup was blood, instead of saying "You are so immature" like he usually would, Jude put some ketchup on his finger, then popped the finger in his mouth and said, "Yum. Tasty!"

Mom cleared her throat. "How was Drama Club today, Ronny?"

"Who?" I replied. My whole family has a bad habit of calling me by that babyish nickname. They'll never learn!

"Oh, sorry," Mom apologized with a smile. "I meant Veronica."

"Drama Club was the best! My teacher looks like an actual real-life movie star! And she's from *England*!"

"Holy cannoli," said Dad.

"That's what I said," I told him. "Also I made a friend named Olivia but we call her Liv, and guess what? I think I made her dreams come true!"

The Show Must Go On

"Sounds fishy," said Jude with his eyebrows raised.

I told them all about Liv's trouble with reading and how I helped. I left out the part where I accidentally made her say stuff about a clogged toilet.

"But how will she read the lines if she gets the part?" asked Jude.

"Oh, silly, silly Jude," I said with a sigh. "She'll just learn them by heart."

"But she'll still have to read them first," he insisted. "She should have a plan. She should make a list."

"You know what this sounds like, don't you?" Ezra asked me.

"A bossy big brother taking over?" I asked.

"Sounds like a job for the Fix-It Friends," Ezra said quickly. Ez is the fastest talker I have ever met.

His mind just goes really fast, and his mouth can sure keep up. It takes a lot of practice listening to him before your ears get quick enough to understand him. I have had lots of practice, so now I'm an Ez-pert. Ha!

"Guys, thanks but no thanks. I don't need help," I replied. "I've got it under control."

"Ooooh, I know what she could do—" Jude started to say. But I had to be firm.

"No, no, no," I interrupted him. "Don't worry your little head about it. You just worry about making the sets. They have to be magnificent! I don't want you to disappoint Ginger Frost."

"Oh, she will not be disappointed," said Jude, pushing his glasses up on his nose. Then he talked on and on about his plans to make swirly sets that seemed really enchanted.

"Miss Tibbs looked at my sketches and said

The Show Must Go On

I might just be the next Vincent van Gogh," he bragged.

"Those are gonna look incredible under my lights!" said Ezra, cracking his knuckles. He always cracks his knuckles when he's on a roll. "I have all these different-colored plastic films to put over the lights so the stage will be different colors at different times. Like, when Alice falls down the rabbit hole, it'll be blue, and when the Queen of Hearts comes out, it'll be—"

"RED!" I shouted.

"Shhhhhhhhh!" Pearl scolded us. "Don' wake up my chicky snuggles!!"

Chapter 7

On Wednesday at dismissal time, I ran as fast as my legs could carry me to the auditorium. I could not wait to see the cast list, to find out who would be playing each part.

I was just turning the corner to the auditorium when *smack*! My head hit something big and black and squishy. I knew right away what it was.

"*Opa!*" I yelped.

Miss Tibbs put her hands on her hips and peered at me through her big black eyeglasses. "Miss Conti."

"Present!" I replied.

The Show Must Go On

"I am not amused." She frowned.

Big surprise. Miss Tibbs is never amused. Irritated, yes. Disappointed, sure. Horrified beyond words, of course. But never amused.

"Sorry, Tiss Mibbs, I mean Mibbs Tiss, I mean Miss Tibbs."

Sometimes she makes me so nervous, I get all tongue-tied.

"How many times have I told you not to run in the halls?"

"Ummmm . . . fifty-seven?" I guessed.

"I don't know how many times. I've lost count."

"Oh, don't worry about it," I said. "I've lost count, too."

I tried to sneak around her so I could get to Drama Club, but she stepped in front of me. Then she gave me a lecture about how lucky it was that I'd crashed into her and not an elderly person, because I could have broken their hip, and how would I feel then? I was sort of confused because I thought Miss Tibbs *was* elderly, but I knew better than to say that to her.

I was really starting to worry about being late to Drama Club when Cora walked by, with her arms full of furry fabric.

"Hi, Miss Tibbs!" squeaked Cora. "I found the fabric you wanted for the White Rabbit."

The Show Must Go On

Miss Tibbs's angry scowl melted when she saw Cora.

"That's perfect, Miss Klein," she cooed.

When she's talking to me, Miss Tibbs is like an angry pit bull, but when she talks to Cora, she's like a newborn chickadee. I know it's Cora's freckles and red hair that do the trick. Sometimes I am tempted to draw freckles on my face and put on a red wig to see if Miss Tibbs would like me then.

While Cora and Miss Tibbs were busy talking about how they'd make bunny ears, I sneaked away. I walked super fast—but I didn't run!—down the hall to the auditorium. I was the last one there!

Minnie, Camille, and Liv were all sitting together, and they had saved me a seat. I sat down next to Liv, who was wearing earrings in the shape of ballet slippers!

As soon as I sat down, I felt someone tap me on the shoulder. Matthew Sawyer, sitting right behind us, whispered, "You're late, you're late, for a very important date."

"Off with your head," I said back to him.

Ginger was walking around in her ruby-red high heels and a big fluffy white turtleneck sweater that looked like a cloud.

"She's giving out the cast list," Camille whispered to me. "And then we're playing improv games."

I didn't have any idea what improv games were, but, knowing Ginger, they'd be super fun.

"Ginger said we won't start reading from the script till next rehearsal," said Liv, who looked relieved.

Ginger handed me the list, and I looked for my name. My heart was thumping so much, I felt like it was an excited chinchilla running around a cage.

It took me a while to find my name because it was at the very bottom.

Queen of Hearts—Veronica Conti

Then my heart felt like a chinchilla doing back-flips!

I read the rest of the list. Camille was playing the White Rabbit. Matthew Sawyer was going to be the Cheshire Cat. Minnie was the musical accompaniment.

And Liv had gotten the part of Alice!

I turned to her and gave her a high five. "You did it! Congrats!"

She nodded, and her blue eyes were twinkling with happiness. But then, all of a sudden, they filled with worry.

"But how am I going to learn all those lines?" she whispered.

That's when I realized four Fix-It Friends are better than one.

"Call your mom during the break and ask if you can come to my house after rehearsal," I told Liv. "I know just who to ask for help."

Chapter 8

Improv is the most fun ever. It is short for *improvisation*, and it means you just make the scenes up as you go along. It is basically the same as just playing pretend. I laughed so much, my belly ached afterward.

Then Ginger said, "Take five!"

"Five what?" I asked.

She laughed her sleigh bells laugh and said, "Five minutes, love. Take a break."

Liv went to the office to call her mom, and I went backstage to find Jude and Ezra. Jude was kneeling down, drawing tree shapes on big pieces of cardboard. Ezra was sitting next to him, in the middle of a big mess of colored plastic sheets.

"I got the part!" I exclaimed.

"Congrats," said Jude.

"Awesome!" said Ezra. He held up a few red plastic sheets.

"Hey, which is better for your entrance?" asked Ezra. "Crimson? Scarlet? Magenta?"

"Umm, they all just sort of look like red to me," I said.

Then I turned to Jude. "What was your big, brainy idea the other night?"

"You'll have to be more specific," he said. "I have a lot of big, brainy ideas."

"The one to help Liv. You were about to tell me at dinner when I told you to can it."

"Ahhh, yes. That was a great idea. One of my best."

"Well," I said, very annoyed, "what was it?"

"Uhhhhh . . . ," he said. "I don't remember."

"Jude!" I shouted.

"Well, I'm sorry, but I forgot! It was a few days ago. Do you have any idea how many ideas I get in a day? I can't possibly keep them all in my brain, or my head would explode."

"It's no big deal," said Ezra. "We'll just think

up another idea. That's why they pay the Fix-It Friends the big bucks."

"No one pays us anything," said Jude.

Ezra chuckled. "Yeah, that's a shame."

Cora walked over then. Her arms were full of purple fur and a pincushion was on her wrist.

"What's going on?" she asked.

"I'm calling an emergency Fix-It meeting after rehearsal today!" I announced.

"So it appears that we, your wise elders, were right about coming up with a plan?" asked Jude.

"Yes, yes, yes!" I snapped. "You were right, okay? You were as right as a math test where you get one hundred percent and three gold stars on the front! So can we have the meeting or not?"

Ezra asked his mom, who is also the principal of our school, and she said sure. Cora was already planning on coming over anyway. All systems go, as my dad says.

After Drama Club, I introduced Liv to everyone.

Ezra held blue plastic sheets up to her face to see which shade was best.

Jude made her stand in front of his cardboard tree to see if it was tall enough.

Cora talked her ear off about costumes. "I was thinking of sewing you an apron to go over your dress. One question: Do you like sequins?"

"One answer," said Liv. "I *adore* them!"

When Dad came to pick us up, he said, "Wow. Full house today, huh?"

But he didn't mind. Dad always says, "The more the merrier." He's a people person, just like me.

When we got home, Dad let us have some of his favorite powdered doughnuts, washed down with hot apple cider. Apple cider is the number one reason I love the autumn. The number two reason is: I love hiding under huge piles of leaves and doing jump scares at Jude.

After the snack, we got down to business.

"Why don't you just tell Ginger about your trouble reading?" asked Ezra. "That's what I would do."

"Me, too," agreed Cora.

"No," said Liv, shaking her head. "I can handle this. I have a really good memory. In a few days, I'll have this whole script memorized. I just need to figure out how to make it through the next few days of rehearsal."

"Oh, I know!" I exclaimed. "Minnie took a ventriloquism class after school one time. What if she sits at the piano and reads your lines without moving her lips, and then you move your mouth, so it looks like you're saying them?"

They all laughed like it was a joke, but I was being serious.

Then Jude asked to see the script. Liv handed it over. She had doodled little pictures of ballet slippers and cats and stuff on the sides of the pages.

"Liv, do you have any trouble looking at pictures?" he asked.

"Nope," she said, "and I don't have a hard time with the very little words like *the* or *me*, stuff like that."

"I know *exactly* what we can do!" Jude said. He took a fresh piece of paper and wrote down Alice's first line in his super-neat handwriting: "A rabbit with a pocket watch? How peculiar!" Then he drew little perfect pictures of a bunny and a pocket watch on top of the words. Jude can draw anything—and fast, too.

When he got to *peculiar*, he was stumped. So he just drew a lot of question marks and exclamation marks.

"Ohhhhh, I get it," said Ezra, looking over Jude's shoulder. "She can read the pictures instead of the words."

Jude nodded and handed the page to Liv. "Try it."

A rabbit with a pocket watch?

?!?!?

How peculiar!

Liv cleared her throat and said, "A bunny with a watch?" Then she looked at all the question marks and shouted very loudly, "WHY OH WHY????"

"It needs a few adjustments," said Ezra. "But not bad."

It took a while for Jude to think up good pictures for the words, so he was able to do only a few scenes. Liv said that was enough for the first rehearsal.

After he was done, Jude and Ezra went into

our bedroom to do homework. I knew I should probably get started on mine, but I just didn't feel like it.

I had a better idea. I turned to Cora and Liv with a smile.

"Death scene, anyone?"

Chapter 9

Liv wanted to try a Devoured-by-Barracuda scene. We turned the coffee table upside down, sat on top of it, and pretended it was a canoe that got sucked into the Bermuda Triangle. I don't know what that is exactly, but I know it's deadly so I guessed it was filled with barracuda.

Our howls were so lifelike that Dad came running into the living room, shrieking, "What happened?" He must have been in the middle of changing Pearl because he was holding her under his arm like a football and she wasn't wearing a diaper.

The Fix-It Friends

Pearl copies everything, so she was shrieking, "What 'appen? What 'appen?"

A few seconds later, the front door flew open and in ran Mom from her office downstairs, where she sees her clients. She was panting from running, and it looked like one of her shoes had fallen off.

"WHO'S HURT?" she yelled.

Two seconds later came my grandparents, who live upstairs.

The Show Must Go On

First came Nana, who carried a fire extinguisher and shrieked, "What's-a da matta?" Then came Nonno. He was holding a baseball bat, and he looked ready to attack.

They all looked really, really funny holding weird stuff and looking so upset, but I knew better than to laugh.

"Everything's fine," I said.

"We're so very sorry," added Cora, who has perfect manners.

"We were just being devoured by barracuda," Liv explained.

Mom didn't say anything. She just smoothed her hair and walked back down the stairs in her one shoe.

"I don't want to rain on your parade," said Dad. "But you need to get devoured a lot more quietly. *Capisce?*"

That's how you say "Got it?" in Italian.

"You-a scared us half-a to-a death!" Nana scolded.

Nonno added, "You almost gave us a heart attack!"

So we stopped the death scenes, and we practiced our splits instead. Liv told me the secret to her success. She says she sleeps in a split! I don't know how she can possibly do that!

Pearl came in, wearing pants this time, and

tried to do a split, too. She lay on her back and stuck one leg up in the air and the other leg out to the side. Then she put her lips together and spit as hard as she could.

"Pearly Pie!" I exclaimed. "What are you doing?"

"Spit!" she cried. "I doin' spits!"

That made us laugh so hard, Dad had to run in again to see if everything was okay.

Chapter 10

At lunch on Monday, I sat next to Minnie and Cora. When Cora unzipped her lunch box, she groaned. Minnie peeked inside.

"Uh-oh," said Minnie. "Looks like a Loco Lunch Box."

That's what we call it when Cora's mom tosses in whole tubs and tins of things that don't really go together. She does it when she runs out of time in the morning, because she is so busy. Mrs. Klein has two different sets of twins. Not just Cora and Camille but also a pair of five-year-old boys, Bo and Lou, who are wilder than a bunch of cheetahs that ate a whole bucket of Halloween candy.

Cora could just get school lunch, like Camille always does. But Cora is a picky eater, and the one part of school she doesn't like is school lunch. So she usually just asks me to trade, and I usually do. After all, I am an adventure lover.

On Monday, when Cora opened her lunch box, she found a half-eaten tub of Marshmallow Fluff, a whole pepperoni, and a butter knife. I love pepperoni, so I traded Cora for some of my bean soup, which Nana calls *pasta fagioli*. Then I shared my saltine crackers with her, and we put marshmallow fluff on top for dessert. Ta-da! Problem solved!

We were munching our marshmallow crackers when Liv walked by our table. I waved her over.

"Did you remember to bring in your picture script?" I asked.

Liv nodded.

"Oh, guess what? I'm going to watch your rehearsal today," Cora said. "Miss Tibbs told me to watch and take measurements."

I whispered, "I don't know how you can stand spending so much time with Miss Tibbs."

"She's so mean," agreed Minnie. "She's always nagging me to stop chewing on my braids—which is just an innocent habit. It doesn't even hurt anyone!"

"Well, it hurts your hair," I pointed out, "and probably your stomach, if you get a hair ball."

"Miss Tibbs is not that bad once you get to know her," squeaked Cora.

Cora likes everyone. Even Matthew Sawyer. Even Bo and Lou, who do hideous things like pull the heads off her Barbies and draw mustaches in permanent marker on her stuffed animals. If she met Snow White's evil stepmother, Cora would probably say, "Oh, she's all right. She just likes to look pretty, that's all."

"Of course you like Miss Tibbs! She loves you more than penguins love ice cubes," I said. Then I imitated Miss Tibbs's voice: "'Miss Klein, what a lovely dress you have. Miss Klein, what lovely

manners you have.' But to me, she's like, 'Miss Conti, what a big mouth you have!'"

"Miss Conti," came a voice right behind me. "I'll thank you to save the acting for Drama Club."

Miss Tibbs had sneaked up on us. I was so embarrassed, I felt my face get red-hot.

"Miss Oikonomopoulous," she said, without even getting one part of that name mixed up. "This is not your assigned lunch table, is it?"

Liv scurried away.

"Will I see you after school, Miss Klein?"

"Without a doubt!" Cora squeaked.

Then Miss Tibbs saw Matthew Sawyer pouring his milk onto his tray and slurping it off with a straw. She ran over to set him straight, as my dad would say.

For once in my life, I thought, *Thank goodness for Matthew Sawyer.*

Chapter 11

Ginger started Drama Club by teaching us some tongue twisters to warm up our mouths so we wouldn't get tongue-tied, like I do with Miss Tibbs.

Ezra was in the auditorium working on the lights, and he did the tongue twisters with us. Because of all his years talking at the speed of light, he was really, really good at them. He could say, "Red leather yellow leather red leather yellow leather" and "She sells seashells by the seashore" at turbo speed, without mixing up any of the sounds!

Then Ginger said it was time to rehearse the

play. Jude was in the wings, painting a gigantic toadstool. I saw him watching Liv nervously to see if his picture script would work.

Great news! It did.

"A rabbit with a pocket watch?" she said. "How peculiar!"

Cora and I were sitting in the front row, and we both gave Liv the thumbs-up sign.

Camille decided her version of the White Rabbit would act like a very successful businessperson—much too busy to stop and talk to Alice. She said, "I'm late! I'm late," in a very rude way, and we all giggled.

When Liv fell down the rabbit hole, Minnie played dramatic music on the piano. She really pounded on the keys. It was so exciting that it gave me goose bumps.

Ginger kept saying stuff like "Smashing!" and

The Show Must Go On

"Brilliant!" Everything was perfect...until Liv got to the part where Alice finds the "Eat Me" cake.

Suddenly, she stopped talking. She looked really closely at the script, squinting her eyes.

I looked at my script, too. She was supposed to say, "Well, I'll eat it! If it makes me grow larger, I can reach the key. And if it makes me grow smaller, I can sneak under the door. So either way, I'll get into the garden!"

Instead, she said, "Well, I'll eat it! And if it burns, I'll swing from a vine. And if it disappears, I'll drive a bulldozer! So yay! I'll get into the dungeon!"

I was very confused. Jude stopped painting sets. Ezra stopped looking through colors for the lights.

Liv gulped loudly. She gave me a look that said, *Yikes! What now?*

I didn't know what to do, so I passed the look over to Jude, who passed the look to Ezra, who passed the look to Cora.

Thankfully, Cora is great at thinking on her feet. She came up with a fast fix.

She jumped out of her seat and ran up onstage, with her long yellow measuring tape hung over her shoulder like a scarf.

"Won't you please excuse me?" she said oh-sopolitely to Ginger. "Miss Tibbs told me I absolutely must get Alice's measurements."

"Right now, love?" Ginger asked. "Can't it wait till the end of the scene?"

Cora opened her big brown eyes extra wide.

"I wish it could wait," she said, her face looking regretful. "But Miss Tibbs said ASAP."

"That means 'as soon as possible,'" I explained.

Ginger closed her script. "All right; it's nearly time for our break anyway. Take five!"

Cora dashed over to Liv and led her into the wings, where she made a big show of measuring her. Jude and Ezra and I walked over.

"What happened with the script?" Jude asked.

"Orange juice happened!" Liv exclaimed, and she handed it to us. Sure enough, something had spilled on the page with the "Eat Me" scene, and the spill had made the pictures all smudged.

They weren't pictures anymore, just big blobs. No wonder Liv was talking about vines and bull-dozers and dungeons!

"I'll just make another one," Jude offered.

Liv shook her head. "It'll take too long."

"I know!" I piped up. "Jude and I will create a distraction. We'll pretend to have a big fight. Jude will call me a rotten lying nincompoop, and then I'll slug him, and then he can kick me in the shins."

The Show Must Go On

Everyone shook their heads and said, "No, no way. Forget it."

Ezra piped up then, talking even faster than usual. "You don't have any trouble learning the words to songs, right? Like, you just hear the words and you repeat them, until you know them by heart, right?"

Liv nodded.

"Okay, cool. So that's what we'll do. I'll record someone reading Alice's lines onto my laptop. I brought it with me to work on the lights. Then I'll send the recording to your mom, and you can listen until you have it memorized."

"Can you really do that?" asked Liv, with wide eyes.

"Are you kidding?" I cried. "Ezra is a computer genius! He's recorded practically my whole demo album!"

Ginger called to us, "Are you about through? We've got to get back to it."

We all nodded.

"It's a great idea, Ez," said Jude. "But right now, she's got to go back to rehearsal, so—"

"I've got to tell Ginger what's going on," said Liv.

"Yep," said sensible Jude.

I sighed. He was right, of course. Every so often, Mr. Know-It-All actually knows something, after all.

Chapter 12

While Liv talked to Ginger, Cora took my measurements.

"I'd like a floor-length gown," I told Cora as she wrapped the measuring tape around my waist and then down my arms and legs. "It should be made of blood-red velvet. Let's put white lace hearts on the front and the sleeves. A velvet cloak with a high collar, too. One that will twirl when I spin around. And of course, I'll need a crown. Fourteen-karat gold would be the best, but if you can only find gold plated, that will probably be okay."

"Uh-huunh," said Cora, looking like she was

picturing every detail. "Or you could wear my long white nightgown with Miss Tibbs's red Christmas apron on top. That's probably the way to go. In fact, it is the only way to go. Miss Tibbs already decided."

"I don't want to wear Miss Tibbs's creepy Christmas apron! She probably wears it to boil bat wings and frog eyeballs."

"Well, you could wear my mom's Hanukkah apron, but it's blue and it just won't match," Cora said as she wrapped the measuring tape around my neck.

"Ahhh, help! I'm choking!" I yelped. "Why are you measuring my neck?"

Cora shrugged. "To tell you the truth, I don't exactly know what I'm supposed to measure. Miss Tibbs figured I already knew how to do it, and I didn't correct her."

The Show Must Go On

"Cora Klein," I said, wagging my finger at her. "Sometimes you are just too polite. You don't have to be perfectly perfect all the time, you know!"

"I know." She sighed and then she said, "You know, I *may* be able to make you a cloak. I found some shiny red fabric in the storage room, and I think it's big enough."

I threw my arms around her.

"You're the best friend and costume designer a girl could have!" I gushed.

"Tell me this: How do you feel about sequins?"

"I feel very good about them." I nodded. "I feel like they are absolutely necessary."

Just then, Liv ran over. She was so happy, she was doing little ballet leaps.

"Ginger wasn't upset at all! She just said she wished I'd told her sooner," she chirped. "I told her about the audition—how you whispered the lines to me—and guess what? That is actually a real job in the theater! It's called being a prompter! And Ginger is going to be standing in the wings during our play in case we need her to do that!"

I was pretty proud that I'd done a real theater job without even knowing it.

Liv also said that Ginger loved Ezra's idea of recording the lines on his laptop. In fact, she said we could spend the rest of rehearsal doing that while she worked on some cat choreography with the Cheshire Cat and Minnie's piano playing.

"I'll ask Miss Tibbs if we can use her microphone," said Cora. "She has one on her desk to make announcements on the loudspeaker."

Miss Tibbs could not say no to her favorite redhead. So a few minutes later, all of us—Liv, Cora, Jude, Ezra, and me—walked over to Miss Tibbs's desk.

Miss Tibbs has an enormous metal desk in the back corner of the main office. Usually, I try to stay far away from it. The desk is very neat, with just a few stopwatches and whistles on top. Most of her stuff is in the drawers—and those all have locks. Who knows what she keeps in there? Maybe torture devices.

"Here you go," said Miss Tibbs as she took the

microphone out of a drawer and locked it right back up. Then she turned to me and said, "I know the precise location of all the items on this desk, and I expect to find them all exactly as I left them. Is that clear?"

"Clear!" I said. Then I gave her a salute like soldiers do. My uncle Eddy is in the navy, and

he taught me how to do it. I thought Miss Tibbs would like that, but she just frowned a lot and walked away.

I read all the Alice lines and all the Queen of Hearts lines. Ezra and Jude and Cora divided up the rest of the parts. The script really wasn't very long, so we were done even before our parents came to pick us up. Just as we were finishing, Ginger walked in.

"Miss Tibbs caught Matthew Sawyer mucking around with the curtains so she's taking the last few minutes of rehearsal to give the cast a lesson on curtain safety," she said. "I reckon she forgot about you, lucky ducks that you are."

She set down a big thermos and stack of cups on Miss Tibbs's desk.

"How about some hot tea on a cold afternoon?"

To go with the tea, Ginger brought biscuits!

Sure, that doesn't sound that exciting, but what you need to know is that in England, *biscuits* means "cookies"!

Ginger's biscuits were called shortbread. They were very buttery and delicious and absolutely perfect for dunking in tea. Could they have used a little whipped cream or Marshmallow Fluff? Of course. But they were pretty good just the way they were.

During teatime, we asked Ginger a million questions.

"Have you ever met the queen of England?" Liv asked.

"'Fraid not," said Ginger. "But a friend of a friend of a friend is her corgis' dog groomer. How d'you fancy that?"

"Oh, I fancy it," I said. "I fancy it a lot. When I grow up, I want to open a dog-grooming business!"

"Do you have a dog?" Liv asked her.

She shook her head.

"Guinea pigs?" Ezra asked. I could tell he was hoping to find a friend for Ziggy.

"No guinea pigs, either. But I've got a tabby cat, Ophelia. She's terribly fussy, but I adore her anyway."

"Is it hard to get your hair in all those twists?" Cora asked. "Do you need a machine?"

It was clear she was thinking of trying the hairstyle on Camille the next time she gave her a makeover.

"They're dreadlocks, love," Ginger replied. "I had them done in a salon. It takes ages, but once they're done, they stay put till you want to be rid of them."

I was a little nervous to ask my question, because I wasn't sure if it was rude or not, but I

figured it was now or never: "Is Ginger Frost your real name?"

She sipped her tea and smiled a big Cheshire Cat smile.

"One of the names is real and one is not. I can't tell you which. I must retain my air of mystery, after all."

The Show Must Go On

"I know! I know! The real one is Ginger!" I guessed.

"No, the real one is Frost," argued Jude. "Definitely."

Ginger just smiled mysteriously. "All I can say is, one of you is right."

"It's probably Jude," I grumbled. "Because Jude's always right."

Jude grinned wide then and said, "You're right about that, at least."

Chapter 13

The next two weeks whizzed by faster than a blood-hound chasing a squirrel. As the day of the show got closer, everyone got busier and busier.

Ezra's lights were amazing! He had a lot of help from Dad, who is a pro at electrical stuff because he's a super in the big apartment building where Ezra lives. Dad even helped Ezra set up a cool spotlight.

Cora was making costumes with Miss Tibbs every day after school and even some days at lunch. She spent a lot of time gluing sequins on stuff. She got a little carried away. When Miss

Tibbs caught her putting sequins on the caterpillar's pipe, she took away her hot-glue gun.

Jude got pretty carried away with the sets, too. He designed them to be so complicated that he couldn't possibly paint them all himself. So, the week before the show, other kids came to help out, even a few of our old Fix-It clients like Noah and Maya.

It turned out that Liv really did have a smashing

memory. At home, she listened to Ezra's recording over and over again, and during our rehearsal breaks, I quizzed her on her lines. After only a week, she had learned them all by heart. Then she offered to quiz me on my lines.

"Thanks, but I don't need any help," I said. "I know my lines."

"Are you sure?" Liv asked. "Because sometimes you *think* you know, but when it's showtime and the bright lights are on you, then it's easy to get stage fright and freeze up. It's happened to me at my ballet performances."

"That happens to me sometimes at my piano recitals," Minnie piped up. "The first time, I didn't know what to do. I was frozen stiff like an ice statue, and my fingers would not move a muscle. But you know what my trick is?"

"What?" I asked.

"I just imagine the audience in their underwear!" giggled Minnie. "Especially polka-dot underwear. It makes me smile and then I feel relaxed."

"That's nice, but I don't get stage fright, trust me," I said. "Hey, listen to the British accent I'm going to use for the Queen of Hearts. I learned it by copying Ginger."

They all loved my accent. Except one person. Guess who did not love it?

Jude, of course. At breakfast, when I asked him to "please be a love and paaaass the maple syrup," he yelled, "MOM! Make her stop! She's driving me to the brink!"

And when I said, "Oh, what rubbish! I'm not driving anyone to the brink! I'm far too young to drive!" he said, "DAAAAAAAD! Do something! She's torturing me!"

After Liv learned her lines, we spent our

rehearsal breaks practicing death scenes. By the time we put on the show, we had nailed down our Poisoned-by-an-Apple scene and Death-by-Whipped-Cream, which was my favorite.

Finally, it was the day of the show. I was so excited that I woke up at 5:30 a.m. and ran straight into my parents' room.

"Today is the day! Today is the day!" I chanted as I threw myself in between Mom and Dad. "Only ten more hours till SHOWTIME!"

"It's *not* day yet," mumbled Dad as he opened one eye. "It's still dark outside."

"Uhhuuuuuh," moaned Mom as she pulled the covers up over her head. She is not a morning person, but I love her anyway.

"But I'm too excited to sleep!" I said, in my best English accent. "I'm full of beans!"

The Show Must Go On

Ginger taught us that expression. It means "jumpy and bursting with energy."

"Make your beans much quieter," grumbled Dad. "And get back to bed."

Chapter 14

I was full of beans all day at school, too. We all were! Cora and I were so nervous that we did our secret handshake about ten times. Minnie chewed on her braids so much, the ends were soggy all day. When I saw Liv at lunch, we threw our arms around each other and screeched, *"Opa! Opa!"* until Miss Tibbs scolded us.

At recess, Jude walked over to where I was playing with my tag gang.

"Here, for the show," he said in an embarrassed way. Then he shoved something small and cold into my hand.

The Show Must Go On

At first, I thought he was pulling a prank on me—like he was going to give me a medal that said WORLD'S BIGGEST PEST or an exploding pen or something. But when I opened my hand, I found a silver chain with a red, sparkly heart attached! A necklace!

My eyes nearly popped right out of my head. There were almost eyeballs rolling around the

playground! I wasn't just surprised; I was shocked. I wasn't just shocked; I was flabbergasted!

"Jude!" I gasped. "I love, love, love, love it!"

He said, "It's not a big deal or anything. I saw it at the toy store with Mom, and it was on sale for practically nothing."

"Not a big deal? NOT A BIG DEAL?" I threw my arms around him and squeezed. "You're the best!"

He shoved me off but I didn't care. I yelled at the top of my lungs, "HEAR YE! HEAR YE! JUDE CONTI IS THE BEST BROTHER IN THE WORLD!!!"

"Why do I do anything nice for you when you are so embarrassing?" Jude said as he walked away, but I thought he looked kind of happy.

I kept rubbing my heart necklace all afternoon and staring at the clock, wishing school was already over. At exactly 3:00, I jumped out of my seat, grabbed my jacket and backpack, and flew out of the room. Cora was right behind me, carrying a bunch of costumes.

I couldn't wait to see Ginger and tell her to "break a leg"! She told us that it's actually *bad* luck to wish someone *good* luck before a play! It's an old theater superstition. You're supposed to say "break a leg" instead!

But when I got to the auditorium, I was in for a shock. Because Ginger was not there.

Yep, that's right.

Ginger!

Was!

Not!

There!

The Fix-It Friends

Do you know who was there?

Right in the middle of the stage?

Miss Tibbs.

"Ummm," I said. "Do you know where Ginger is?"

I held my breath and hoped with all my might that Miss Tibbs would say, "Oh, she's just running a little late" or "She's in the bathroom." But

instead, Miss Tibbs said four terrible words: "She has the flu."

I gasped. I could not believe my ears. Then Miss Tibbs said more terrible words: "I'll be filling in for her."

I gasped again. I couldn't help it! It just slipped out.

"You appear to be troubled, Miss Conti," said Miss Tibbs. "Are you all right?"

I nodded really fast.

"Then quickly get into your costume," ordered Miss Tibbs. "Guests will be arriving in thirty minutes."

Chapter 15

I grabbed my Queen of Hearts costume, and Cora and I dashed into the bathroom to change. A second later, Liv walked in, carrying her Alice costume.

"Did you see Miss Tibbs?" she asked. "Can you believe our rotten luck?"

"Our luck's so rotten, it's got a worm crawling in it!" I exclaimed.

"What if I forget my lines?" said Liv. "Ginger was going to be the prompter."

"You won't," Cora said. "You're so prepared!"

The Show Must Go On

Then Cora tied the sash on Liv's dress and spun her around.

"You look fantastic!" squeaked Cora.

Liv was wearing one of Cora's dresses, which was light blue with poofy short sleeves. On her head was a blue silky headband that exactly matched her eyes. She wore black ballet slippers on her feet. She had changed her earrings to little blue gemstones that glittered in the light.

Then Cora frowned and tugged on one of her curls. "But where's the apron I made for you?"

Liv looked down and said, "Oh yeah. Well, the thing is, my mom washed it, and it got all torn up in the machine. I'm sorry about that."

Oooooh, I knew she was lying! The reason I knew that is, I had thought of telling the exact same lie to Cora about the cloak she'd made for me.

The Fix-It Friends

It turns out that even though Cora is great at nearly everything, she is not very good at sewing. That's putting it nicely. The truth is, she is horrendous! If you blindfolded Pearl and tied one arm behind her back, she would still do a better job sewing than Cora. My friend might know a lot about fashion, but one thing she does not know is how to make it.

I saw the apron that Cora made for Liv before it went missing. The top part was so short that Liv had to tie the belt right under her armpits. Not only that, but the bottom part was much too long, way longer than the blue dress underneath.

But even though the apron was terrible, it was a hundred times better than my cloak. My cloak had too many problems to list. Here are just a few:

1. The neck was so tight, I could hardly swallow.

2. It dragged on the floor—which would have been cool, except it dragged on only one side.

3. The other side was even shorter than my knees.

4. She used black thread instead of red thread, so you could see all the stitches, which were big and crooked. It looked like a Franken-cloak.

5. There were a billion red sequins but only on one side because when she was halfway through with it, Miss Tibbs took away her hot-glue gun.

Nana could have fixed the cloak on her sewing machine in about two minutes because Nana used to be a professional seamstress. But Cora was so proud of her work, and I knew her feelings would be hurt if I changed it or if I lied that a pigeon had swooped down and grabbed it out of my hands. So I wore that Franken-cloak on show day.

The rest of my costume looked great. Cora's white nightgown with Miss Tibbs's red apron looked nice (after Mom washed it twice to get rid of witch germs). Nana had bought me a plastic crown, and it fit perfectly. And of course, I had my supremely amazing showstopping necklace that my BBF (best brother forever) got for me.

Liv, Cora, and I rushed back to the auditorium and checked out everybody else's costumes.

This is what Camille wore as the White Rabbit:

1. White sweatpants with a big white furball pinned to her butt.
2. A headband with furry bunny ears sticking up.
3. A white T-shirt with white furry sleeves sewed on by Cora. One sleeve

reached to her elbow, and the other sleeve reached past her wrist. They were both hanging on by just a thread.

Minnie looked lovely in the outfit she always wears to recitals—a silky white shirt, black velvet pants, and a white headband with her hair in two braids. The ends were still wet, but you couldn't really notice.

Then I saw Matthew Sawyer and my mouth dropped open. This was what he wore as the Cheshire Cat:

1. A striped shirt, as usual, but this one had light purple and dark purple stripes.

2. Purple sweatpants.

3. Lavender face paint with a big clownish smile painted on in dark purple.

4. My friend Maya's pink kitty hat from Tokyo, with adorable pink kitty ears sticking up.

In the middle of his huge face-painted smile, his real mouth was in a big frown. I couldn't help but giggle. I'm only human, after all!

When Matthew Sawyer heard me laugh, he got furious.

"Oh, just zip it," he hissed. "Haven't you ever seen a kid dressed like a cat before?"

The Show Must Go On

"Sure, but never one in such an adorable hat!" I teased.

"Forget it!" he exclaimed. "I'm not listening to any more of this."

Then he turned around to storm off. And when he did, I saw that a long purple tail was swinging from his butt.

That did it. I burst out into huge chortles.

"Miss Conti, if you're done with your laughing fit, maybe you'd like to get into your place in the

wings?" Miss Tibbs asked. "The doors are opening now for our guests."

The red curtain was supposed to be closed so we could open it when the show started like in a real theater, but Matthew Sawyer had broken it by mucking around and it didn't close anymore. So I had to stand in the wings and peek out to see the audience. Absolutely everyone was there! Jude was sitting right in the front row, and next to him were Mom and Nana and Nonno and Dad, with Pearl on his lap. Ezra was not sitting with them, because he had to sit in the back of the auditorium to control the lights, but his mom, Principal Powell, was there, at the end of the row.

Liv's mom was there, and next to her was a very jolly-looking man who I guessed was Liv's dad. He had a big round belly like Santa Claus, with big furry eyebrows and absolutely no hair on his head at all.

Minnie's moms were in the second row next to Cora's parents and the twins Bo and Lou, who were poking each other with sticks. Maya was there with her mom, and so were Noah and his teenage babysitter, Ivy, who had a green streak in the front of her hair.

"All right, actors," whispered Miss Tibbs. "It's showtime. I'd like to wish you all good—"

"NO!" I yelled at the top of my lungs.

"Miss Conti!" Miss Tibbs looked so mad, her eyes bulged.

"Ginger said you should never, ever tell an actor good luck before a show," I stammered.

Liv agreed. "She said we should say 'break a leg!'"

Miss Tibbs closed her eyes and sighed really loudly.

"All right, then. Break a leg," she said. "But don't really break a leg, or an arm, or a collarbone, either. There have been two broken arms this month at recess, and I don't wish to add to the list."

Chapter 16

The play was a smash hit! It will go down in theater history!

Liv did not forget one single line. Not one.

There was someone who did forget her lines.

Me!

I never thought, in a million years, that I would get stage fright, but I did! Just like Minnie and Liv had warned me.

I walked onstage and the lights were so bright, I felt blinded. Then I started to feel really, really hot. I felt like I couldn't breathe normally.

I opened my mouth to say my first line, but no

words came out. All of a sudden, I had absolutely no idea what I was supposed to say! I opened and closed my mouth a whole bunch of times. I must have looked like a fish.

I heard a familiar voice yell, "HI, WONNY! HI, WONNY! PWETTY WONNY!" I squinted into the first row and saw Dad stick a pacifier into Pearl's mouth to keep her quiet. Mom gave me a thumbs-up. But it was like someone had pressed PAUSE on my brain, and I just could not think.

Thankfully, Liv flew to the rescue. She did a pirouette, and while she spun around, she whispered, "What is your name, child?"

It was like she had pressed the PLAY button on my brain. Suddenly, I remembered everything I was supposed to say.

"What's your name, child?" I said in my jolly good British accent.

The Show Must Go On

The audience laughed, and that let me know I was doing a great job, so after that, I wasn't nervous anymore.

I shouted "OFF WITH HER HEAD!" louder than ever before. After I yelled it, I heard Pearl shriek "OFF WIFFER 'ED!" a few times until Dad popped the pacifier back in her mouth.

There were a few other wee problems, as Ginger would say. Liv was supposed to do a bunch of pirouettes when Alice falls down the rabbit hole, but she lost her balance and knocked over one of Jude's swirly green bushes. Matthew Sawyer was hiding behind that bush, ready to pop out as the Cheshire Cat. So not only did Liv bash Matthew Sawyer in the head, which made him scream, "HEY! Watch it!" but she also broke the bush, which made Jude scream, "No! Not my bush!" Someone else yelled, too. It was Liv's dad, and he shouted, "*Opa!*"

The Fix-It Friends

And then there was the problem with Camille. She was worried about forgetting her lines, so she wrote them all along her arm. Halfway through the play, she pulled up her sleeve so she could read her arm, and when she pulled the sleeve back down afterward, she yanked a little too hard. It fell right off.

When she leaned over to pick up her sleeve,

her bunny-ear headband slipped off her head and fell right off the stage. She should have just left it there, but she didn't. Quick as a flash, she hopped off the stage to grab the bunny ears. And *that's* when she broke her leg.

Well, she didn't break it, really. She just twisted it. But Miss Tibbs made a big deal out of it anyway.

"I knew I shouldn't have told you all to break a leg!" she grumbled as she helped Camille limp backstage. We had to call an emergency intermission while Matthew Sawyer's mom, who is a doctor, examined Camille. Even though she didn't break her leg, it still hurt her a lot, so Dr. Sawyer told her to sit out the rest of the play.

Lucky for us, Cora looks exactly like Camille, so she just slipped on Camille's costume and did the part. She had to hold her script, and she was wearing only one sleeve, but it was still pretty good. As Ginger always said, the show *must* go on.

When the play was over, we got a standing ovation! We all bowed together—even Camille, who limped back onstage for the curtain call.

When I was standing there on the stage, holding Liv's hand on one side and Camille's hand on the other and listening to all those people clap and cheer, I felt so full of happiness, like a hot-air balloon floating through the clouds.

Afterward, Liv's dad rushed over. He gave Liv and me a huge bear hug and lifted us off the ground.

"The famous Veronica Conti!!" he cheered. "I've heard all about you—and the rest of these Fix-It kids. You were lifesavers, you know that?"

"Thanks, but the truth is, Liv was the lifesaver

today," I said, turning to her. "If you hadn't told me my line, I'd still be standing there, with my big old fish mouth."

She laughed. "It's no big deal. Everyone needs a little help sometimes. Even you."

Just as Liv's family was leaving, Mom and Dad walked over, carrying a big bunch of red roses.

"We didn't even have to paint them red," joked Dad.

Nana was smiling and wiping her eyes. Nana is a big crier. When she is happy or proud, she instantly tears up.

"You-a are *una stella vera*!" she sniffled. "A true star!"

"There goes Nana with the waterworks!" Nonno joked. Then he asked me to autograph his program.

Pearl begged and begged to wear my crown and cloak, so I let her. Then she pretended to be the Queen of Hearts for the rest of the night and kept yelling "Off wiffer 'ed!" to Ricardo. She loved that cloak so much, she refused to take it off. So I guess Cora has one fan, at least.

Chapter 17

I was feeling like it was the absolute best day ever—even better than my birthday or Christmas. And then Miss Tibbs walked over to me.

I tried to think of what I'd done that had got me into trouble. Was it because I ran down the hall to the auditorium after school? Was it because I was chewing gum while I ran? Was it because I was yelling "Show day! Show day!" while I chewed gum and ran?

But she didn't scold me or lecture me. In fact, she smiled at me and handed me an envelope.

"Congratulations," she said.

Guess what was inside the envelope?

A homework pass! Which means that one night, whenever I want, I can have NO HOME-WORK!!

Instead of slaving away and breaking pencils,

The Show Must Go On

I'll just lie on the sofa and eat marshmallows and watch cartoons. And when Jude passes by to get a new pencil because he's used up all the pencils at his desk because he has sooooooo much homework, I'll just say oh-so-casually, "Oh, it must be a tough homework night. I wouldn't know. I have a homework pass."

And I will be thinking, *Eat your heart out, big shot! Ha!*

"I was very impressed by the way you helped Liv with her script," Miss Tibbs said.

I nodded.

"And I think you were the perfect person to play the Queen of Hearts," she went on. "Do you know why?"

"Because I like to boss people around and yell at the top of my lungs?" I asked.

She shook her head.

"Because you have one of the biggest hearts of anyone I know," she said.

I threw my arms around Miss Tibbs without even thinking. As soon as I realized what I had done, I jumped backward. I was sort of embarrassed. But Miss Tibbs just seemed happy.

"I know you had a little help," she said, and she handed me three more envelopes that said MR. CONTI and MR. POWELL and MISS KLEIN.

"Will you make sure they get these?" she asked.

For a second, I considered keeping them for myself. Then for a few more seconds, I considered just keeping Jude's for myself. But then I remembered the heart necklace.

"Absolutely," I told Miss Tibbs.

* * *

The Show Must Go On

A few days later, at dismissal time, Miss Mabel handed out bright red papers again—but this time, just to the Drama Club kids.

"It's a letter!" squeaked Cora. "From Ginger!"

Here is what it said:

I was terribly disappointed to miss the show! I heard from everyone, including Miss Tibbs, that it was an absolute smash! But I didn't just take her word for it. Liv's father was kind enough to record the performance. I have watched the video three times, and here is what I think:

You did it, loves! You made magic. You transformed that auditorium into a Wonderland. You did it by working together: listening to each other and looking out for each

other. You were true collaborators. I'm terrifically
proud of you. Well done!

Big hugs,
Ginger Frost

I pressed the letter to my heart and grinned. Then I looked at it again, and I saw something written at the bottom, underneath her name. It was a handwritten note, just for me.

Veronica,
I know your brother's almost always right about
everything, but you were right about my name.
Ginger's the real part. My name's Ginger Butte.
Yes, I know. It's dreadful.
P.S. You must keep acting. You're a natural.
Today, the Queen of Hearts. Tomorrow, Lady
Macbeth!

Take the Fix-It Friends Pledge!

I, (say your full name), do solemnly vow to help kids with their problems. I promise to be kind with my words and actions. I will try to help very annoying brothers even though they probably won't ever need help because they're soooooo perfect. Cross my heart, hope to cry, eat a gross old garbage fly.

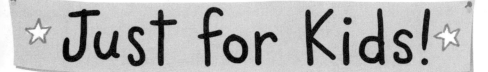

Just for Kids!

What's in Your Reading Toolbox?

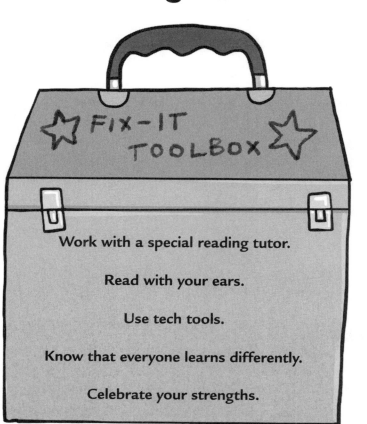

FIX-IT TOOLBOX

Work with a special reading tutor.

Read with your ears.

Use tech tools.

Know that everyone learns differently.

Celebrate your strengths.

When Reading's a Real Struggle...

Reading's a big challenge for a lot of super-smart kids—and grown-ups, too! There are a few reasons why reading might be tricky, but the most common explanation is something called dyslexia. People who are dyslexic don't hear sounds in words as easily as other people, which means they have a hard time matching letters to the sounds those letters make. Because of this, reading can be really tough.

How does it feel?

"I like reading a lot, but when I come to a big word that I can't figure out, I get really, really stressed. Like I want to yell, 'Ahhhhh!'"

—Zola, age nine

"It makes you feel dumb. You feel like you can't do anything."
—**Chloe, age twelve**

"It's really hard for me to read the words, so I only read if I have to. I would read for one minute if I could have an hour of computer time."
—**Sean, age eight**

What helps?

"If you're stuck on a word, keep on reading and then you can figure out the word that you missed. Also, take a break, calm down, and then go back to reading later when you're not as stressed out."
—**Lanie, age ten**

"I look for patterns or rules, like the silent *e* rule, or the *vccv* pattern, or compound words."
—**Zola, age nine**

"I use my hands to only see that word on a page. Bigger text helps, because there's more space in between words."

—Chloe, age twelve

"Slowing down and breaking up the word helps. Don't hesitate to read out loud. If you get something wrong, you just move on."

—Ethan, age twelve

What to Do When Reading's Really Hard

Ready to hear something that might surprise you? Tons of people have dyslexia—about one out of every five people! In fact, lots of your favorite athletes, movie stars, musicians, and other world-famous, super-successful folks are dyslexic. Ever heard of a guy named Steven Spielberg? Muhammad Ali? Tom Cruise? Yep, they're all dyslexic. Reading was really hard for them when they were kids, but they didn't let it stop them from dreaming incredible dreams and working hard to achieve them. Guess what? It won't stop you, either! You just need the right kind of help.

1. Work with a special reading tutor.

For some kids, learning to read the way most people do, by sounding out words, just doesn't work very well. The great news is, there are other ways to read. Your parents or school can find a special reading tutor for you, someone who's an expert in special reading systems. The tutor will teach you awesome strategies like how to break words down and find patterns in them; before long, reading will start to make a lot more sense.

2. Read with your ears.

Reading print books can be tough, but listening to audiobooks—which are read aloud by people—well, that's a whole different ball game. Whoever said you need eyes on paper to read, anyway? You can listen to just about anything—not just books, but also magazines, websites, and even homework!

3. Use tech tools.

Audiobooks are just the tip of the iceberg when it comes to technology that can be helpful. If handwriting's a big problem, you can type on a keyboard. If spelling's stopping you in your tracks, you can dictate your work to an electronic device. If taking notes in class is the challenge, snap a picture of the blackboard with a camera.

4. Know that everyone learns differently.

Some people with dyslexia have said that their difficulty with reading made them think they weren't smart. This could not be further from the truth! In fact, most people with dyslexia are really smart. Dyslexia does *not* mean that you don't learn as well as other kids; it just means you learn *differently*.

And everyone learns in slightly different ways. Some people learn best by hearing information, others by seeing it, and others by moving their bodies around or by working in groups.

If you need things that other kids don't—extra time on a test, to get reading material in advance, to use a tech tool—don't waste a second worrying about how that makes you different from the rest. After all, anyone who is extraordinary is always different.

5. Celebrate your strengths.

People with dyslexia are some of the most curious, creative, talented people around. They're amazing at solving problems in new and exciting ways because their dyslexia has given them plenty of practice doing just that.

Remember, if something's important to you—whether it's scoring the lead in the school play or writing a book—you can absolutely achieve that goal. Just be creative, stay determined, and get the right people in your corner to help! Like the Disney saying goes: "If you can dream it, you can do it."

Want more tips or fixes for other problems? Just want to check out some Fix-It Friends games and activities? Go to fixitfriendsbooks.com!

Resources for Parents

If your child is struggling with reading, these resources might be helpful.

Books for Kids

The Alphabet War: A Story about Dyslexia by Diane Burton Robb and Gail Piazza, Albert Whitman & Company, 2004

It's Called Dyslexia by Jennifer Moore-Mallinos, Barron's Educational Series, 2007

Thank You, Mr. Falker by Patricia Polacco, Philomel Books, 2012

Books for Parents

The Dyslexic Advantage: Unlocking the Hidden Potential of the Dyslexic Brain by Brock L. Eide, MD, MA, and Fernette F. Eide, MD, Hudson Street Press, 2011

The Dyslexia Empowerment Plan: A Blueprint for Renewing Your Child's Confidence and Love of Learning by Ben Foss, Ballantine Books, 2016

Overcoming Dyslexia: A New and Complete Science-Based Program for Reading Problems at Any Level by Sally Shaywitz, MD, Vintage, 2005

Websites

Bright Solutions for Dyslexia

www.brightsolutions.us

Dyslexia help from the University of Michigan

www.dyslexiahelp.umich.edu

For parents of dyslexics

www.dyslexichelp.org

International Dyslexia Association

www.interdys.org

LD Online

www.ldonline.org

Understood: For Learning and Attention Issues

www.understood.org

Xtraordinary People

www.xtraordinarypeople.com

Yale Center for Dyslexia & Creativity

www.dyslexia.yale.edu/dyslexiastraighttalk.html

Don't miss the next adventure of

The Fix-It Friends

Wish You Were Here!

About the Author

Nicole C. Kear grew up in New York City, where she still lives with her husband, three firecracker kids, and a ridiculously fluffy hamster. She's written lots of essays and a memoir, *Now I See You*, for grown-ups, and she's thrilled to be writing for kids, who make her think hard and laugh harder. She has a bunch of fancy, boring diplomas and one red clown nose from circus school. Seriously.

nicolekear.com